04616

WITHDRAWN

Wanda Gág's

JORINDA

and

JORINGEL

illustrated by Margot Tomes

COWARD, McCANN & GEOGHEGAN, INC.

NEW YORK

LIBRARY OF CONGRESS CATALOGING IN PUBLICATION DATA

Grimm, Jakob Ludwig Karl, 1785–1863.
    Wanda Gág's Jorinda and Joringel.

    Translation from the German by W. Gág of J. L. K. Grimm's
and W. K. Grimm's Jorinde und Joringel. Text originally
appeared in the collection More tales from Grimm.

    SUMMARY: When a witch changes Jorinda into a nightingale,
her sweetheart Joringel discovers through a dream how to
save her.

    [1. Fairy tales] I. Gág, Wanda, 1893–1946. II. Tomes,
Margot. III. Grimm, Wilhelm Karl, 1786–1859, joint author.
IV. Title. V. Title: Jorinda and Joringel.

PZ8.G882Wan   [398.2]   [E]   77-26680
ISBN 0-698-20440-9

Printed in the United States of America
Typography by Cathy Altholz

To Betty Main

I don't know if it is still there, but at one time there was an old grey castle in the middle of a deep, dense forest where lived an old woman who was a witch. By day she took the form of an owl or a cat, but after sundown she always became a human being again. She had many cruel tricks but the one she liked best was her Magic Circle Enchantment, for with this she could catch anyone who came within a hundred steps of the grey wall surrounding her castle.

If it was a man or boy who strayed beyond this danger line, he became rooted to the ground and could neither move nor talk until the Old One chose to disenchant him. If it was a young girl who stepped within the Magic Circle, the old enchantress turned her into a bird, packed her into a covered basket and carried her into a great hall inside her castle. And you can see how great was her wickedness when I tell you that in her home she already had seven thousand such baskets, each containing a captive bird which had once been a maiden.

Now it happened that in this forest, and not far from the witch's domain, there lived two young friends who loved each other dearly. One was a girl and her name was Jorinda. The other, a boy, was called Joringel.

One balmy summer evening these two set out for a stroll in the woods. Hand in hand they went, as was their wont, and all about them everything was calm and beautiful. The birds twittered and fluttered among the leaves. The sunbeams slanted between the tree trunks and fell in shining ribbons against the dark green of the forest. The two children were peaceful and happy.

"How beautiful it is!" said Joringel. "But we must be careful not to wander into the witch's Magic Circle."

"Oh, we can't be near it yet," said Jorinda light-heartedly; and so they walked on, watching the rabbits and squirrels, picking a flower here and there. But before long their happy mood dwindled away.

The leaves began to rustle mournfully, the birds became quieter and quieter. Jorinda and Joringel, they knew not why, grew silent and solemn. On and on they walked, slowly now, and with heavy steps. A turtle dove was singing its song among the beeches, and the children became strangely sad. Tears rolled down Jorinda's cheeks; Joringel was filled with a nameless woe. Confused and forlorn, they looked for the way home but could not find it.

"Oh, I think we are lost!" said Joringel, and Jorinda knew he was right.

The sun was sinking fast. One half of its

glowing face still showed above the rim of a distant mountain top, the other half had already dropped out of sight.

Joringel, searching for a path, spied something grey showing between the twigs of a tall thicket and became alarmed, for he knew this could be only one thing: the grey stone wall of the witch's domain. Jorinda seemed to notice nothing and was acting strangely. In the fading light she had sunk down on the grass and now she was singing, almost sobbing:

> *My birdie with the red, red ring*
> *Cries sorrow, sorrow, sorrow.*
> *It sings the end of everything.*
> *Oh sorrow, sorrow, sor — tsick-eet!*
>   *tsick-eet!*
>   *tsick-eet!*

Joringel turned quickly and looked at Jorinda.
In the midst of her song she had changed into
a singing nightingale with a beautiful red ring
around her throat; and now an owl with
glowing eyes and a sharp, hooked beak was
flying over them.

Three times the owl circled over them,
and three times she screeched,

"Shoo hoo! hoo! hoo!"

Joringel could not move; he stood there motionless as a stone—could not walk, could not weep, could not talk. The sun sank behind the mountain top—then it was gone. The owl disappeared behind a thicket, and in the next moment out came a bent old woman carrying a

covered wicker basket. Yellow and haggard she
was, with big red owlish eyes and a beak-like
nose which almost touched her chin.

Muttering to herself, she caught the little
nightingale who had once been Jorinda,
clapped the bird into her basket and hobbled
off toward the old grey castle, cackling
happily.

As her footsteps rustled off among the leaves, darkness closed in dusky folds over the forest, and Joringel, standing speechless and motionless as before, was left alone. But although he could not speak, he was still able to think well enough, and what he thought was: "That was the old witch, and she has taken my dear little Jorinda into her grey castle forever!"

Before long the Old One returned and, standing before Joringel, chanted in a hollow voice:

> *Greetings, Zachiel, now to thee!*
> *When the little moonbeams fall*
> *On the basket in my hall,*
> *Loose this lad and set him free.*

When Joringel heard these strange words he was puzzled. He did not know who this Zachiel might be, but he soon guessed the meaning of the rest of the song, for suddenly, as the moon stole out from behind a cloud, he found he could move and talk once more. Knowing himself to be freed, he now wished to free Jorinda also, so he fell on his knees before the old sorceress and begged her to release his playmate.

But the Old One said, "You'll never get her back."

Joringel pleaded and prayed and sobbed—it was all in vain. With a triumphant cackle the Old One turned her back on him, hobbled away and soon was out of sight and hearing.

"Oh, what will become of me now?" moaned the boy. He made his way out of the forest and, dazed with sorrow, wandered off until he

came to a strange village. Here he hired
himself out as a shepherd and herded sheep for
many a long month.

At last, one night, he had a dream. He dreamt he found a red, red flower, in the heart of which lay a wondrous pearl. Plucking the flower, he walked without fear to the grey castle where all that he touched with the flower became disenchanted, and in this way he freed his dear Jorinda.

That was his dream.

When he awoke the next morning, he set out to search for such a magic flower. Up the steep mountains he went, through villages and valleys, and into the depths of tangled woodlands. For eight days he wandered thus, and on the morning of the ninth day he found a red, red flower! In its rosy blossom-cup nestled a morning dewdrop, laughing and sparkling and more beautiful than a pearl.

Carefully he plucked the flower and carefully he held it too, as he walked day and night until he reached the witch's forest.

When he came within a hundred paces of
the witch's domain he did not become rooted
to the ground as before. Instead, he walked
up to the ponderous gate and touched it with
his red, red flower. The gate sprang open and
Joringel walked into the courtyard, listening
for the sound of the birds.

Yes, he could hear something—a thousand-
throated twittering and trilling and warbling.

But where were the birds? Where in that big castle was the great hall in which the Old One kept the seven thousand enchanted maidens and his dear Jorinda-nightingale? Entering the castle on tiptoe, Joringel made his way toward the warbling sounds, and at last, after winding his way through a maze of chambers and corridors, he came upon a large hall from which issued the music and fluttering of myriads of birds.

The door of the room was ajar and Joringel peered in. What a sight he beheld! On the floor, on the walls, on the shelves and tables and chairs and benches, were seven thousand birds in seven thousand baskets; and there, too, was the old sorceress busily feeding her flock of songsters. As Joringel paused at the door, wondering what to do next, the Old One looked up. When she saw him her face twisted up in fury and then, spitting poison and gall with each step, she advanced threateningly toward him. But Joringel was not to be frightened so easily. Quickly he held out his red, red flower, and as he did so the old sorceress was forced to stop; and when she found she could not get within two steps of him, she fumed and screamed and scolded.

Joringel took no notice of her. He had other things to do, and his only thought was for his beloved Jorinda. She was somewhere in the room; he must find her and free her. From basket to basket he went, peeping into every one of them in search of his nightingale. But just as there were hundreds of canaries, hundreds of song sparrows, hundreds of wrens, thrushes, swallows and linnets in the baskets, so there were hundreds of nightingales too. How

would he ever be able to tell which one of these was Jorinda? While he was searching, he kept an eye on the Old One too, and suddenly, out of the corner of his eyes, he saw that she was up to some mischief. She had ceased scolding and screeching, had stealthily picked up one of the baskets and was now trying to sneak off with it toward another door.

"That looks queer!" thought Joringel, acting quickly. Leaping in front of her, he touched first the cage, then the witch, with his red, red flower. As he did so, the Old One lost all spirit and stood defeated and limp before him,

for now she was powerless and could never enchant him or anyone else again. In her hand she held an empty basket, and in front of him stood Jorinda, a nightingale no longer, but a girl with happy dancing eyes and arms outstretched in welcome.

"Oh Jorinda!" cried the boy. "Now we can go home and be happy together as before. But wait! I have a pleasant task to do before we leave," and, going all around the room from basket to basket, he touched each one with his magic flower. And—oh wonder and joy!—as he did so, one bird after another stopped singing, the lid of each basket popped open, and out of every one sprang a happy, grateful maiden.

Yes, now all of the seven thousand baskets were empty, and seven thousand lovely maidens crowded the great hall, curtsying and thanking Joringel for freeing them. And then, leaving the old sorceress alone and powerless in her big gloomy castle, the maidens returned to their homes and lived happily ever after; and Jorinda and Joringel did the same.

WANDA GÁG translated 52 of Grimm's fairy tales, although she had not completely illustrated *More Tales from Grimm* at the time of her death in 1946. Ms. Gág was posthumously honored with the Lewis Carroll Shelf Award in 1958 and the Kerlan Award in 1977.

MARGOT TOMES has illustrated more than 30 books for young readers, many of them for Coward, McCann. She chose *Jorinda and Joringel* from Wanda Gág's collection of Grimm's tales for her first full-color artwork, which was done in ink and gouache. Ms. Tomes' drawings for *Jack and the Wonder Beans*, by James Still, was cited as one of the Best Illustrated Children's Books of 1977 by the New York Times Book Review.

The text was set in Fairfield, the title type was hand-lettered, and other display type was set in Caslon 471. The book was printed by offset at Rae Lithographers.